The Boy of Color

THE BOY OF COLOR
Copyright © 2006 Kids' Club North America, NFP.

Published in Nashville, Tennessee, by Tommy Nelson®, a Division of Thomas Nelson®, Inc.
Visit us on the Web at www.tommynelson.com.
Tommy Nelson® books may be purchased in bulk for educational, business, fund-raising,
or sales promotional use. For information, please email SpecialMarkets@ThomasNelson.com.

A special thanks goes to Jeff Foster, art teacher at Kids' Club, for his help on this book.

            Library of Congress Cataloging-in-Publication Data
Nelson, Sherrie, 1990–
  The boy of color / Sherrie Nelson ; illustrations by Joquese Cantrell.
      p. cm.
  Summary: A young boy who loves to paint and draw turns to God for help
when he runs out of inspiration.
  ISBN-13: 978-1-4003-0910-8
  ISBN-10: 1-4003-0910-7
  1. Children's writings, American. [1. Color—Fiction. 2. Artists—Fiction. 3. Christian
life—Fiction. 4. Children's writings. 5. Children's drawings.] I. Cantrell, Joquese,
1991– ill. II. Title.
  PZ7.N4368Bo 2006
  [E]—dc22
                              2006005971

Printed in China
06 07 08 09 10 MT 5 4 3 2 1

THE BOY OF COLOR
Copyright © 2006 Kids' Club North America, NFP.

Published in Nashville, Tennessee, by Tommy Nelson®, a Division of Thomas Nelson®, Inc.
Visit us on the Web at www.tommynelson.com.
Tommy Nelson® books may be purchased in bulk for educational, business, fund-raising,
or sales promotional use. For information, please email SpecialMarkets@ThomasNelson.com.

A special thanks goes to Jeff Foster, art teacher at Kids' Club, for his help on this book.

ISBN-10: 1-4003-0910-7
ISBN-13: 978-1-4003-0910-8

Printed in China
06 07 08 09 10 MT 5 4 3 2 1

The **Boy** of **Color**

by
Sherrie Nelson

Illustrated by
Joquese Cantrell

Tommy NELSON®

A Division of Thomas Nelson Publishers
Since 1798

www.thomasnelson.com

Kids' Club—Growing a Future and a Hope
A Word About This Book and the Kids Who Wrote It . . .

Surrounded by poverty, gangs, and violence, it's difficult for a child to imagine the future. Yet, that's exactly what Sherrie Nelson and Joquese Cantrell did as they walked from their respective schools through Cabrini-Green—one of Chicago's largest and oldest housing projects, and at one time the most dangerous, having more murders occur per square foot than anywhere else in the nation. Sherrie and Joquese walked with a purpose, heading past boarded-up windows, burned-out apartments, and paved open spaces.

They headed to Kids' Club. Founded in 2001 and piloted with sixteen children, Kids' Club is a faith-based after-school program that nurtures the whole child—mind, body, and soul. Due to its success, it now serves hundreds of children from first through twelfth grades—all recommended by principals as "children in critical need for intervention." More than a conventional learning program, Kids' Club mentorship is focused on helping high-risk inner-city children have a chance at a new, abundant life. As the children each begin to realize their special purpose as a unique creation of God, they begin to realize their hopes and dreams.

For three years Sherrie has been a member of Kids' Club. Joquese has been a member for nearly a year. Together, they have written and illustrated *The Boy of Color*. Sherrie, the oldest of five children, is a sophomore at Best Practice High School. She hopes to be a pediatrician when she grows up, enjoys writing because it helps her express her feelings, and hopes children who read *The Boy of Color* will learn that God loves them no matter who they are. Joquese, the oldest of four children, is an eighth grader at Manierre School. Joquese wants to be a surgeon when she grows up, enjoys drawing as a pastime, and hopes that children who read *The Boy of Color* will learn they can do anything.

Portions of the royalties from *The Boy of Color* are being donated to Kids' Club to help other children discover bright and hopeful futures. For more information about Kids' Club, see the website at www.kidsclub.ws.

Once there was a boy named Blue.
Blue loved colors.
Coloring and painting were his
favorite things to do.

He colored with crayons, markers, paints, and pencils of **all** colors.

He **loved** to color . . .

. . . draw pictures . . .

. . . paint portraits . . .

. . . and **design** his own clothes.

But **one** day, Blue ran out of things
to do with his colors.

He decided to ask everyone in
his family what he should do.

He went to his father, and his **father** said, "Boy, do as you please."

He went to his mother, and she said, "**Follow** your heart."

He went to his big sister, and she said,
"I don't know. Leave me alone!"

Blue was disappointed. These were
not the answers he was hoping for.

So Blue went to his room
and lay on his bed.

Staring up at his ceiling, Blue
thought about what he should do.

He began to pray, "God, what should I do with my colors?"

And God gave him the answer he was looking for.

Red is for love because **hearts** are red.

Yellow is for JOY because the sun is always bright and full of joy.

Blue is for **peace** because rivers are blue, and the Bible talks about having "peace like a river."

Green is for **patience** because nature is green, and it is mostly calm and **steady**, never getting in a hurry.

Purple is for faith because mountains are purple, and to have faith, you have to stand like a mountain.

Black is for self-control because darkness is black, and when we go through dark times, we have to trust in God and practice self-control.

And orange is for gentleness
because autumn is orange . . .

. . . and after the hot days of summer
and before the cold days of winter,
autumn is the gentlest time of year.

God let Blue know he was the Boy of Color.

And he was to teach others what to
do when they saw his colors.

And most importantly, Blue was to
remind others that God created
all colors and that they are
all beautiful . . .

. . . especially people of different colors.